The Story of
Santa's Birds

This Book Belongs to

Dedicated, in alphabetical order, to Andrew, Bruno, Louise, and Rosemary.

Inspired by the lore of Rosemary Koning.

Brought to life on long walks with London the Leonberger.

The Story of
Santa's Birds

By Kyle and Cheryl Koning

Illustrated by Fanny Liem

Long before winter's snows,

someone is watching and someone knows.

But it is not a man who drives a sleigh.
Someone else is watching every day.

6

In olden days while making toys,

Santa could watch the girls and boys.

He saw them playing, he saw them run,
he saw them laughing and having fun.

8

But towns becames cities
and buildings grew tall.

How could Santa
see them all?

9

"Who is naughty?
Who is nice?

I can't check once,
let alone twice!"

10

"I need some help to check my list.

Someone who can never miss."

11

"Who can watch
them all year round?

Who can float,
above the ground?"

12

"Who can see them play together?

Perhaps I can ask someone with . . .

. . . feathers?"

13

"The birds can help,"
Santa cried,

"they can watch
while they fly!"

"I need your help,"
he said to the flock,

"to watch the kiddies
all 'round the clock."

15

"To look for mischief
and to look for trouble,

then report what
you see, on the double!"

16

Robin and Jay said,
"We'll watch in the Spring!"

"I'll help too," tweeted Finch,
"I won't miss a thing!"

17

"Summer's our season," said Gull with a screech,

"Sandpiper and I will watch from the beach!"

"We'll take Autumn," croaked Raven and Crow.

19

"Winter for me," sang Cardinal, "I love the snow!"

20

"For farms and fields you can count on me!" Pheasant cried.

21

And Parakeet chirped,
"I'd like to help too and
watch from inside!"

22

"We Pigeons can cover the city and park,
but who can we get to spy after dark?"

"I know!" said Santa, "I'll ask old Mrs. Owl.
She can keep watch whilst out on the prowl."

24

"I thank you, Birds, for your help to see.

How can I reward you for spying for me?"

25

"All your children can help us,"
cooed the peaceful Dove,

"ask them to give us
the seeds that we love!"

26

"Or a tiny apartment," suggested the Wren,

"with an outdoor bath in a lovely garden!"

27

"It's settled!" said Santa
with his eyes agleam,

"Welcome, all Birds,
to my Behavior Team!"

28

And his Birds flew off
to watch and spy

on all of the children
they could see from the sky.

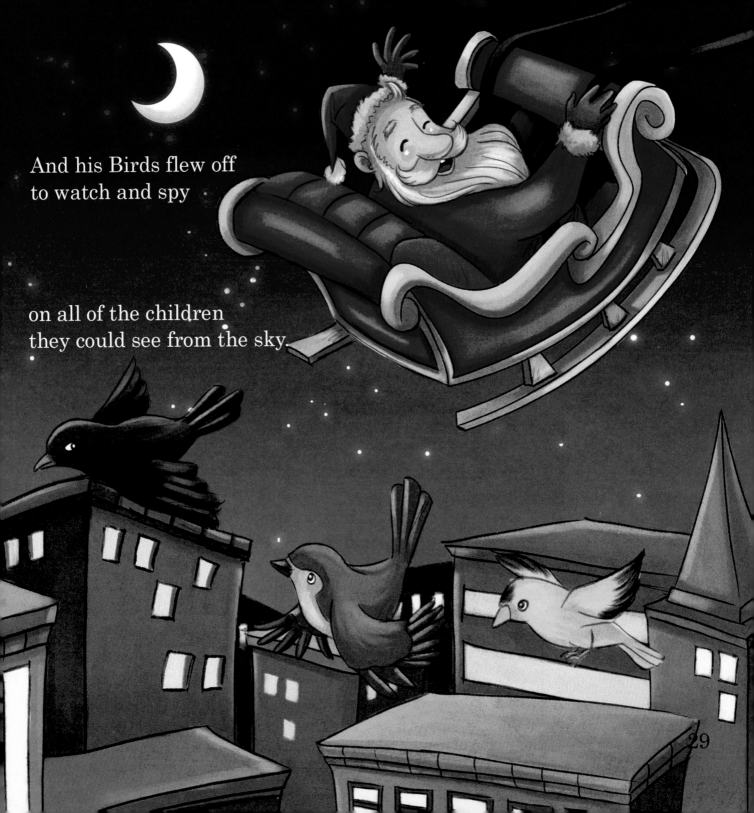

Those same birds are watching to see if you're good,
so remember to always do as you should.

Stay out of trouble and don't be a pest!

For they see you from trees
and from inside of their nests!

31

They sit on rooftops and atop the ledge.

They're on the fence and they're in the hedge.

The Birds tell Santa
what they discover,

so follow the rules and
be good to each other.

33

Remember this story
and mind these words,
for they are outside watching . . . they are Santa's Birds!

34

Want to learn more about the Birds on Santa's Behavior Team?

Visit us on the web at www.SantasBirds.com for
information on birds, fun bird-related activities, and
interactive projects to help the birds in your neighborhood.

About the Authors

photo by Brittany Erin Photography, San Francisco, California

Kyle and Cheryl Koning are a husband and wife writing team living in San Francisco. They live far away from their families and while reminiscing about holiday family traditions they decided to share the secret of Santa's Birds with the world. Even though they cannot always be home for the holidays, they know that Santa's Birds are keeping an eye on all of us to see if we are good.

Made in the USA
Lexington, KY
14 November 2017